To All My Old, Old Saddle Pals

There's hardly a trail we didn't roam,

But the sun is setting in the West,

And it's time for me to head on home.

COWBOY DREAMS

BY
DAYAL KAUR KHALSA

CLARKSON N. POTTER, INC./PUBLISHERS
NEW YORK

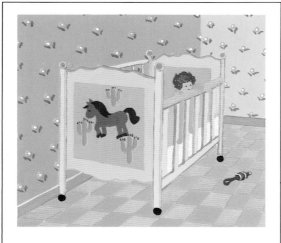

When I was a girl I wanted to be a cowboy.

My earliest memories are of lying on the living room rug, listening to "The Lone Ranger" on the radio. "Hi Ho, Silver! Away!" were practically the first words I ever said.

All day long I made believe I was a cowboy. I galloped everywhere, slapping my thigh and yelling, "Giddyap!" to make myself go faster. As I grew older I developed a bowlegged walk and tied my blankets into a bedroll at the foot of my bed. My whole life revolved around being a cowboy. I called my bike Old Paint, my brother Pardner, my supper chuck and my bedroom the bunkhouse. Whenever I went on a merry-go-round I pretended I was out riding with a posse, chasing bandits.

Of course, I knew very early that if I were ever going to be a real cowboy, I needed a horse.

Whenever my mother took me to the Metropolitan Museum of Art I would look long and thoughtfully at my favorite painting, trying to decide what kind of horse to get.

At the Main Street movies on Saturday afternoons I studied how to be a cowboy, watching every move my cowboy heroes made. I learned how to dash from hedge to hedge in a crouch, how to tip my hat back and squint into the sun, how to leap onto my rolling bike and how to ambush anything and anyone. All week long I practiced jumping out at my mother, brother, grandma and the cat.

When Tony the Pony Man came to our block I sat as tall and brave in the saddle as Hopalong Cassidy.

I had been asking for a horse for my birthday since I was three years old. But my parents didn't even want a dog in the house and I knew, deep down, they would probably never get me a horse. I bought a raffle ticket to win one.

I planned how to convert our garage into a stable. My mother said to my father, "With my luck, she'll win the horse." I kept my fingers crossed and hoped with all my might that she was right.

D ay after day I ran home from school to see if the mailman had brought me a letter saying I'd won. Weeks, and then months, went by. The letter never came. I tried hard to content myself with riding the mechanical horse in front of Eli's store . . . dreaming of life in the Wild West. I wished I was a horse wrangler or the scout for a wagon train.

To cheer me up my grandma took me to F.A.O. Schwarz, the best toy store in the world. There I saw the horse of my dreams. It was almost as big as a real horse and it had wheels. I knew that if I had a horse like that, I could be a cowboy. I begged her to buy it for me. She told me that expensive toys like that were meant only for the children of kings and maharajas. Oh, how I wished my father was a maharaja! But he was a tailor—and I wasn't going to get that horse.

So when it became too cold to ride Old Paint and Eli put his mechanical horse into storage for the winter, I built myself a horse on the basement banister. I made stirrups from a piece of clothesline and the little cardboard tubes that come inside rolls of toilet paper. I used a jump rope for the reins. I folded a blanket for the saddle.

All winter long, I spent hour after hour riding my banister horse and singing my favorite cowboy songs. Songs that would carry me away, into the world of my dreams, into the land of the cowboys . . .

Oh, give me a home where the buffalo roam, where the deer and the antelope play,

Where seldom is heard a discouraging word and the skies are not cloudy all day.

I'm a poor, lonesome cowboy,
I'm a poor, lonesome cowboy,
I'm a poor, lonesome cowboy
And a long ways from home.

I ain't got no sister,
I ain't got no sister,
I ain't got no sister
To go and play with me.

I ain't got no brother,
I ain't got no brother,
I ain't got no brother
To drive the steers with me.

I'm a poor, lonesome cowboy,
I'm a poor, lonesome cowboy,
I'm a poor, lonesome cowboy
And a long ways from home.

As I walked out in the streets of Laredo,
As I walked out in Laredo one day,
I spied a poor cowboy wrapped up in white linen,
Wrapped up in white linen as cold as the clay.

"I see by your outfit that you are a cowboy."
These words he did say as I boldly stepped by.
"Come sit down beside me and hear my sad story;
I am shot in the breast and I know I must die.

"Get six jolly cowboys to carry my coffin;
Get six pretty maidens to sing me a song.
Take me to the graveyard and lay the sod o'er me
For I'm a young cowboy and I know I've done wrong."

From this valley they say you are going,
I shall miss your sweet face and bright smile.
For they say you are taking the sunshine
That has brightened my pathway a while.

And, you know, every once in a while I find myself humming one of those old sweet songs—and I feel as bold and brave and free as a cowboy again. *Giddyap!*

Published by Clarkson N. Potter, Inc., and distributed by Crown Publishers, Inc.,
201 East 50th Street, New York, New York 10022

CLARKSON N. POTTER, POTTER and colophon are trademarks of Clarkson N. Potter, Inc.

Manufactured in Japan

Library of Congress Cataloging-in-Publication Data

Khalsa, Dayal Kaur.
Cowboy dreams/Dayal Kaur Khalsa.
p.   cm.
Summary: A little city girl wants to grow up to be a cowboy.
[1. Cowboys—Fiction.]   I. Title.
PZ7.K52647Co   1990   [Fic]—dc20   89-22782
ISBN 0-517-57490-X
Glb 0-517-57491-8
10   9   8   7   6   5   4   3   2   1

First Edition